When 10-year-old Ben Tennyson stumbles upon a mysterious alien device in the woods one summer, little does he realise that his life is set to change - forever.

As soon as the watch-like Omnitrix quite literally gets a grip on him, Ben discovers it gives him the ability to transform into 10 different alien super-beings, each one with awesome powers!

Using the Omnitrix to cause super-powered mischief turns out to be fun, but will Ben learn to use his might to fight for good?

READ ON AND FIND OUT . . .

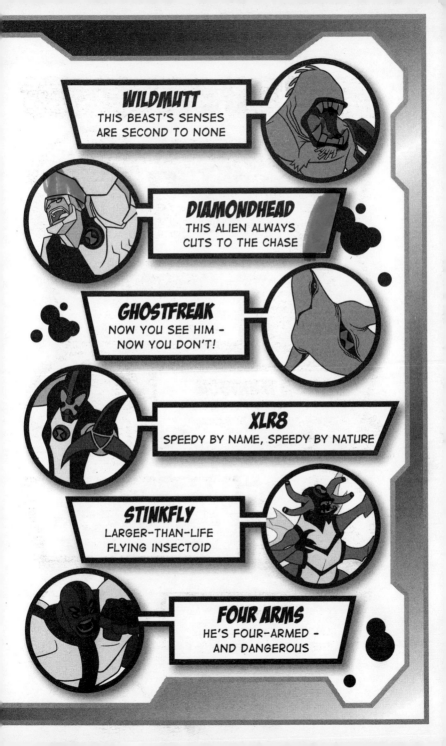

EGMONT
We bring stories to life

Published in Great Britain 2008
by Egmont UK Limited
239 Kensington High Street, London W8 6SA

Ben 10 and all related characters and elements
are trademarks of and © Cartoon Network.
(s08)

Adapted from the animated series by
Barry Hutchison

ISBN 978 1 4052 4467 1

5 7 9 10 8 6

A CIP catalogue record for this title is available from
the British Library

Printed and bound in Great Britain by the CPI Group

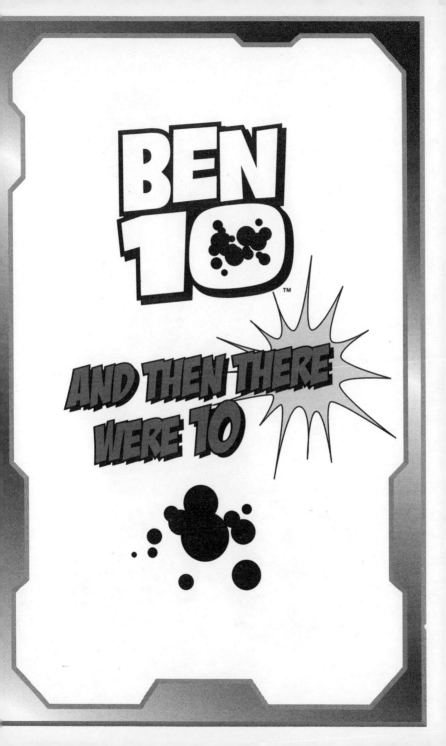

CHAPTER ONE

MEET BEN TENNYSON

In the dark depths of outer space, a small alien spaceship dodged and weaved through a meteor shower. It spun and twisted to avoid the energy blasts of a much larger battleship that followed close behind.

BLAM! The smaller ship was suddenly thrown sideways as one of the blasts slammed into it. A direct hit!

The ship opened fire with its own weapons and burned two deep holes in the side of the battleship.

On board the monstrous battleship, a black-and-red robot studied the flashing lights on the computer screen. The smooth metal walls of the ship shuddered as another energy blast exploded against the outside.

'Hull damage, twenty per cent,' said the robot in a mechanical voice. 'Weapon systems still operational.'

Behind the robot, a huge, hulking alien leaned forwards in his command chair and narrowed his red eyes. Although he was half hidden by shadow, it was possible to make out his slimy green skin, his bald head and the row of tentacles that stuck out from his chin like a

beard. His name was Vilgax, and he was very, very angry!

'I have come too far to be denied!' the evil alien growled. He bunched his hands into fists. 'The Omnitrix shall be mine and there is not a being in this galaxy that dares stand in my way!'

❈ ❈ ❈

Meanwhile, in a classroom many millions of miles away, a boy named Ben Tennyson was hard at work. He was focusing his full attention on the sheet of paper on his desk, folding it over and over again.

The folding was finished and his masterpiece was complete. After making sure no one was watching, Ben picked up his paper aeroplane and launched it across the classroom.

He watched it swoop over the desks. He watched it float past the open window. Finally, he watched it curve sharply and crash, nose first, against the back of his teacher's head!

By the time the teacher had turned round, Ben had snatched up a book. He hid behind it, pretending to be reading, until she turned her attention back to the blackboard. Phew! That was too close!

The rest of the lesson seemed to go on forever. It was the last day of school before the summer, and all Ben could think about were the holidays. He and his grandpa were off camping – just the two of them. It was going to be great!

Eventually, the end of the day drew near. Ben sat perched in his seat and watched the final few seconds tick away. Ten seconds until the bell. Five seconds. Four, three, two, one!

BRRRRRRRRRRRING! The moment the bell started to ring, Ben leaped from his seat and rushed for the door.

'Yesss!' he laughed. 'I'm outta here!'

'Benjamin?' said the teacher sternly.

'Could I have a word with you before you go?'

Ben stopped mid-run and turned round. He swallowed hard when he saw the teacher was holding his paper aeroplane.

'Uh-oh,' he gulped. 'Busted.'

�֎ ✖ ✖

A few minutes later, with his telling off still ringing in his ears, Ben finally escaped from school. He strolled through the playground, enjoying the sunshine, but enjoying his freedom even more. School was over. The holidays were just beginning. Good times lay ahead!

Ben turned a corner and spotted two older kids pushing a much smaller boy around. Ben recognised the younger boy as Jamie from his class. The bullies laughed as they shoved him hard against a tree.

'Normally we'd take your money and beat you up, but since it's the last day of school we're gonna give you a break,' snarled one of the bullies. He held out a dirty hand. 'Now hand over the cash!'

Jamie quickly reached into his school bag. If it meant he wouldn't get beaten up, he was happy to hand over any money he had.

'Leave him alone!'

The bullies spun round to find Ben standing nearby. They laughed when they saw him. Not only were they bigger than he was, but there were two of them and only one of him.

'Get lost, shrimp!'

'I said,' growled Ben, 'back off!'

'Looks like we got us a hero,' said the other bully. Both of them advanced menacingly. 'Suppose we don't want to back off?'

The bullies were almost upon Ben now. One of them leaned forwards as he spoke. 'What are you going to do about it, Tennyson?'

Ben narrowed his eyes and clenched his fists. It was time to teach these guys a lesson!

At least, that was the plan. Instead, Ben soon found himself dangling from a tree branch by his underwear. Jamie hung helplessly from the next branch over – another victim of the bullies' famous Atomic Wedgie!

'Thanks,' Jamie sighed. 'Thanks a lot!'

Shuddering, shaking and spitting out clouds of black smoke, a tatty motorhome stopped just outside the school gates. A friendly-looking old man wound down the window and leaned his grey-haired head out.

'Come on, Ben, let's go. We're burning daylight,' he shouted over. 'I want to make it to the campsite by nightfall.'

Ben rolled his eyes. 'Uh, Grandpa,' he called, 'a little help here?'

✸ ✸ ✸

Grandpa Max climbed back into the motorhome. The floor creaked and groaned as he made his

way to the driver's seat. He didn't call the van
The Rust Bucket for nothing!

Ben hopped inside, still adjusting his
underwear. He pushed the door closed behind
him and followed Grandpa.

'I've been so looking forward to this,'
he grinned.

He stopped in his tracks as he realised
they were not alone. His cousin, Gwen, was
sitting at The Rust Bucket's dining table.

'What are *you* doing here?' he demanded.
He spun back to face Grandpa Max. 'What is
she doing here?'

'Take it easy, dweeb. This wasn't my
idea,' Gwen explained. 'Somebody convinced
my mom that going camping for the summer
would be a good experience for me.'

'I can't *believe* it,' Ben moaned. 'I wait
all school year to go on this trip and now the
Queen of Cooties is along for the ride!'

'Hey, I had my own vacation already

planned out too, ya know,' replied Gwen. 'Now
I'm stuck with my geekazoid cousin going
camping for *three months*!'

'Geek,' Ben snapped.

'Jerk,' Gwen spat back.

Up at the front, Grandpa Max turned in
his seat and started the engine. With a splutter,
The Rust Bucket wheezed into life. As it pulled
away from the school, Grandpa sighed quietly.

'Something tells me it's going to be a long
summer.'

CHAPTER TWO

GOING HERO

Ben and Gwen sat at a picnic table, surrounded by hundreds of tall trees. They had arrived at the campsite just as the day was drawing to an end. It was dark now, with only their campfire to light up the night.

'Chow time!' Grandpa announced. He stepped down from The Rust Bucket holding a large plate. Ben sniffed the air. Dinner smelled fantastic! He hadn't realised until now how hungry he was.

But not *that* hungry. Ben stared down at the slimy mass on the plate Grandpa had set before them. Whatever it was, it looked disgusting. What was worse, it was moving!

'OK, I give up,' he said, watching helplessly as half his dinner began to crawl across the table. 'What *is* that?'

'Marinated mealworms,' announced Grandpa proudly. 'They're considered a delicacy in some countries.'

'And totally gross in others,' Gwen scowled.

'If these don't sound good, I've got some smoked sheep's tongue in the fridge.'

Neither option sounded appealing to Ben. 'Couldn't we just have a burger or something?'

'Nonsense!' laughed Grandpa. 'This summer is going to be an adventure for your tastebuds.' He turned and headed back towards the motorhome. 'I'll grab the tongue.'

'OK,' whispered Ben, leaning in close to his cousin, 'I got a half-eaten bag of corn chips and a candy bar in my back pack. What you got?'

'Some rice cakes and hard candy.'

Ben nodded. It wasn't much, but it was better than worms. 'Think we can make them last the whole summer?'

※ ※ ※

In outer space, the two ships were still locked in battle. Their laser blasts were slower now, and it seemed the fight was almost over.

Vilgax's robotic second-in-command scanned the controls. 'Their propulsion systems have been destroyed,' it announced.

'Prepare to board,' barked Vilgax. 'I want the Omnitrix now!'

Before the robot could react, an energy blast exploded against the hull. Vilgax roared with rage as shards of glass and metal rained down on him.

Furious, he flipped open a panel on his chair. He managed to stab a clawed finger into the controls and activate the ship's most powerful weapon before another explosion hit the command deck.

A bolt of pure energy shot from the front of Vilgax's ship. It tore through the smaller ship as if it were made of paper. With a blinding flash, half of it was turned to specks of space dust.

Unseen by Vilgax, a hatch slid open in the belly of the shattered spacecraft. A small, round pod emerged and streaked off towards a distant blue-and-green planet.

The planet Earth!

✖ ✖ ✖

Down on that very planet, Ben was walking in the forest near the campsite. He'd had enough of Gwen already, and needed some time by himself. Why did Grandpa have to bring her along? This was going to be the worst summer ever.

A movement overhead caught his eye. He looked up and saw a bright light streaking across the sky.

Ben stopped walking and watched the sparkling light. It seemed to be getting brighter. Brighter and bigger. Much, *much* bigger. At the last possible moment he realised the shooting star was shooting straight for him!

Ben threw himself out of the way just as the ground where he'd been standing exploded with a deafening **BOOM!** Large lumps of rock were thrown up into the air, and the whole area was covered by a choking cloud of dust.

When the smoke had cleared, Ben edged forwards. The meteorite had left a large, round crater in the middle of the forest. He crept closer and saw a small metal ball resting at the bottom of the hole.

Before he could figure out what the thing was, to his alarm the ground at Ben's feet crumbled. He slid down into the crater and skidded to a stop right next to the sphere. It hissed slightly as it opened, revealing an eerie green glow.

Ben leaned in closer. There was something inside the ball – something very un-alien.

'A watch?' he frowned. 'What's a watch doing in outer space?'

Without warning, the weird device leaped out of its protective shell. It wrapped round Ben's wrist and clamped on tight.

'Get it off! Get it off!' he shouted, frantically trying to shake the thing off his arm. He grabbed on to the black strap and heaved, but it wouldn't let go. The watch was stuck!

Ben pulled himself up out of the crater and staggered off in the direction of the

campsite. He yanked at the watch, still trying to take it off. No matter how hard he tried, though, it continued to cling on.

He studied the thing more closely. He couldn't see how he was supposed to tell the time with it. There were no hands on it at all. Instead, it displayed some strange symbols, with three green rings round the outside.

As he fiddled with the device, it suddenly let out a loud **BLEEP!** The middle of the watch raised slightly. Ben's eyes widened as a figure shaped like a man appeared on the display.

'Cool!'

He pushed the raised part of the watch back down. Instantly, a strange green energy swirled from it and snaked up his arm. As the energy passed across him, Ben felt his body begin to mutate.

First his arm bulged and grew, then his skin turned red and rough as rock. The changes quickly travelled over his shoulder,

up his neck and began to sweep across his face. He closed his eyes, terrified, as the transformation took hold.

When Ben opened his eyes, he was no longer quite himself. He looked down at his new body. He was adult sized and bright red from head to toe – however, something even stranger than that had happened: every single part of him was covered in flames! He didn't know it yet, but Ben had become an alien called Heatblast.

'I'm on fire! I'm on fire!' he cried, before he realised the flames weren't hurting him.

'Hey, I'm on fire and I'm OK!'

Heatblast glanced at a nearby tree. *Hmm*, he thought, *I wonder*.

He pointed to one of the lower branches. A blast of flame shot from his fingertip and blasted the wood to pieces.

'Now *that's* what I'm talking about!'

He squeezed his hands together. An orange flame flickered between them. It grew and grew until it became a swirling ball of fire.

The fireball shot from Heatblast's hands and ripped through a row of trees, snapping them in half. As the trees fell, the heat from the fireball ignited their leaves. They were still burning when they hit the ground.

'Wait! Stop!' yelped Heatblast, but it was too late. As the smouldering leaves hit the grass, the blaze quickly took hold. Within moments the damage was done.

The forest was on fire!

CHAPTER THREE

A FLAMING DISASTER

'What's that?' asked Gwen, pointing towards a bright glow in the sky above some nearby trees.

'Looks like the start of a forest fire,' Grandpa replied. 'We'd better let the ranger station know. Probably some darn fool camper out there messing around with something he shouldn't.'

Grandpa and Gwen stood in silence for a few moments, considering this. A terrible thought occurred to them both.

'Ben!'

'Better take this,' said Grandpa, throwing Gwen a fire extinguisher. After snatching up one for himself, they both set off in the direction of the glow.

❈ ❈ ❈

In the heart of the forest, Heatblast was trying desperately to stamp out the fire. But every time his foot touched the ground, his flames set something else alight. This fire was getting well and truly out of control!

Even though the flames were close enough to burn him, Heatblast couldn't feel them. He should have been in agony, but the fire didn't hurt a bit.

'This would be cool if it weren't so *not* cool,' he mumbled to himself.

Suddenly, a blast of white foam hit him in the face. He coughed and spluttered, choking on the chemical spray. Blinded for a moment, he staggered and almost tripped.

When his eyes had cleared, Heatblast

found himself face to face with Gwen. Foam dripped from the nozzle of her fire extinguisher. She stared up at the alien for a few seconds, and then screamed at the top of her voice.

'I know I look weird,' Heatblast said, trying to calm her down, 'but there's no reason to be scared . . .'

But it wasn't Gwen who needed to be scared. Recovering quickly from her fright, she swung the heavy fire extinguisher with all her strength. It made a loud **CLANG** as it glanced off Heatblast's head. The force of the knock sent him tumbling to the forest floor.

Gwen raised the nozzle of the extinguisher and pointed it at the fallen alien. 'I don't know what you are, but you'll stay down there if you know what's good for you,' she warned.

Annoyed, Heatblast launched a few bolts of flame at Gwen's feet. She yelped with fright. One of her shoes had caught light! Hopping like mad, she blasted her foot with the fire extinguisher, then turned back to the alien. She held the extinguisher up, ready to deliver another crunching blow.

'I warned you!' she growled.

The alien's eyes narrowed. 'Don't even think about it, freak.'

That last word stopped Gwen in her tracks. 'Freak'. There was only one person who ever called her that.

'Ben?' she gasped. 'Is that you? What happened?!'

Taking a deep breath, Heatblast hurriedly filled her in on everything. He was just reaching the part where he'd accidentally set the forest on fire when Grandpa Max came running up.

'Gwen, are you all . . .' he began. He stopped when he spotted Heatblast. 'What in blazes?'

'Hey, Grandpa,' said Gwen, 'guess who?'

'It's me, Grandpa!'

'Ben?' frowned Grandpa. 'What happened to you?'

'Well, when I was walking, this meteor –'

'Um, excuse me,' Gwen interrupted, 'major forest fire burning out of control, remember?'

Heatblast and Grandpa looked around. The blaze now surrounded them.

'What do we do?'

Grandpa thought for a few moments. 'Backfire,' he said at last. 'Start a new fire and let it burn into the old fire. They'll snuff each other out.' He turned and looked at the blazing figure next to him. 'Think you can do that, Ben?'

'Shooting flames I can definitely do!'

He turned and ran straight for the nearest wall of flame. Without hesitating, Heatblast jumped through the fire. He kept running until he was standing in an untouched area of forest. Any second now the flames would reach these trees too. There was no time to lose.

Concentrating hard, Heatblast threw out his hands. He felt a hot surge of power build up inside him. It quickly shot along his arms. In a burst of blinding light, a jet of flame leaped from his fingertips.

The closest trees immediately caught alight, and it only took a few seconds for the new fire to take hold.

Heatblast turned off his flame-thrower fingers and watched anxiously. What if the plan didn't work? The blaze was spreading fast. What if, instead of solving the problem, he'd made things worse? He chewed his lip nervously. The plan had to work. It had to!

YESSS! Within minutes, the two fires met and began to snuff each other out. He'd done it! Heatblast had saved the day! With a little bit of help from his Grandpa, of course.

❋ ❋ ❋

Vilgax was hurt, but he was alive. Just. He had lost more than half his body when the command deck had exploded. Now he floated in the yellow liquid of a Medi-Tube, breathing through the ship's life-support systems. His body would regrow, but it would take time.

'This battle nearly costs me my life,' he wheezed, 'and you say the Omnitrix is no longer on board the transport?'

His robotic second-in-command lowered

its polished head. 'Sensors indicate a probe was sent out from the ship just before boarding,' it explained. 'It landed on a nearby planet.'

What was left of Vilgax's face twisted into a scowl. 'Go,' he commanded. 'Bring it to me!'

❊ ❊ ❊

Heatblast watched a marshmallow go brown in his hand. Within seconds it had dissolved into a squidgy goo. He popped it in his mouth. Mmm, tasty!

'And you say that this "watch" just jumped up and clamped on to your wrist?' asked Grandpa. They were sitting around the campfire and watching carefully to make sure nothing else went up in smoke.

'Hey, this time it wasn't my fault, I swear,' Heatblast insisted.

'I believe you, Ben,' nodded Grandpa.

'Think he's going to stay a monster

forever?' asked Gwen. Part of her secretly hoped the answer would be 'yes'.

'He's not a monster – he's an alien,' Grandpa replied. He realised Gwen and Heatblast were staring at him quizzically. 'I mean look at him,' he added quickly. 'What else could he be?'

'I don't want to be fire guy forever!'

'Don't worry, Ben, we'll figure this thing out.'

They all jumped with fright as the watch gave a loud **BLEEP!** Heatblast stood up as a few more beeps rang out. Just as the last one sounded, he was lit up by a bright, blinding flash.

Ben looked down at himself. His hands were his own. His clothes were his own. Even better, he was no longer on fire!

'I'm me again!' cried Ben. He gave the watch an experimental tug. 'But I still can't get this thing off.'

'Better not fool with it any more until we know exactly what we're dealing with,' warned Grandpa. He stood up and headed for the forest. 'I'll go check out the crash site. You guys stay here until I get back.'

Gwen and Ben watched him disappear into the trees. Neither of them noticed the sleek shape that sliced silently down from the sky above their heads.

CHAPTER FOUR

GIVE A DOG A DRONE

The robot stood at the edge of the crater, scanning for any sign of the Omnitrix. Its sensors soon detected the metal shell, but immediately realised it was empty. Someone had taken the watch! This was not good.

It raised a hand and unleashed a blast of energy. Instantly, the shell was reduced to a smoking pile of melted metal.

Two hidden compartments in the robot's shoulders unfolded, allowing a pair of spinning discs to fly free. They whizzed through the forest and, as they flew, a set of sharp metal claws extended below them both.

The robot watched them zoom off into the

trees. If the Omnitrix was nearby, they'd find it. It was only a matter of time.

❋ ❋ ❋

Ben sat with his back against The Rust Bucket, fiddling with the watch. He pressed, pushed, twisted and pulled, but he couldn't figure out what made the thing tick.

'Caught ya!' Gwen yelled. She burst out laughing when she saw how much she'd startled her cousin.

'Very funny,' Ben snapped. 'Like your face.'

'Grandpa said not to mess with that thing,' she reminded him.

'Come on,' said Ben, 'you can't tell me you aren't a little bit curious about what else this thing can do.'

'Not in the least.'

Ben looked her up and down. 'Are you

sure you're related to me?' He turned his attention back to the watch. 'Look, if I can figure this thing out, maybe I can help people. I mean really help them, not just, you know, make things worse.'

Despite herself, Gwen couldn't help but be curious. 'So what did it feel like,' she asked, 'going all alien like that?'

'It freaked me out at first,' replied Ben. 'It was like I was me, but also like I was somebody else.' He twisted the outside ring of the watch. With a **BLEEP!** the centre raised up once more. 'Hey, I think I've figured out how I did it,' he said. 'Should I try it again, just once?'

'I wouldn't.'

'No, duh,' Ben mocked, '*you* wouldn't.'

He slammed his hand down on the watch, and was immediately swallowed up by the cloud of weird energy. This time, though, there were no flames. Instead, Ben felt millions of thick, wiry hairs burst through his skin. Fangs as large as carving knives tore up through his bottom jaw, just as sharp claws sprouted from his fingers and toes. With an animal roar, Ben transformed into the savage Wildmutt!

'Eww!' Gwen winced. 'This thing's even uglier than you are normally. Bow wow, put a flea collar on this mutt.'

Wildmutt opened his mouth to reply, but all that came out were some strange grunts and groans.

'And no eyes?' scoffed Gwen. 'What good is this one? It can't see!'

A wicked thought suddenly occurred to her. Moving stealthily, Gwen picked up a stick and crept over to the huge, dog-like alien. She raised the stick like a cricket bat, then swung it, full speed, towards Wildmutt's butt.

The blind alien cocked his head. Its senses detected the threat, and powerful leg muscles sprang into action. Gwen gasped as the creature backflipped out of danger. The Rust

Bucket creaked and shook as Wildmutt landed on its roof.

'OK, so maybe it's not a total loser,' Gwen admitted. The alien leaped down from the motorhome and landed in front of her. She pulled away, covering her nose with her hands. 'Two words,' she choked, 'breath mints!'

Wildmutt snorted, then turned away. He kicked his back legs, spraying Gwen with mud and grass, before bounding off into the trees.

'Ben, get back here! Ben! I'm gonna tell Grandpa that you turned into some freaky animal-monster thing and went swinging around the forest when he told you not to.' She replayed her entire last sentence in her head. 'This,' she sighed, 'is a majorly weird day.'

�֎ ✦ ✦

Wildmutt swung and leaped from branch to branch. He flipped and spun through the forest, easily jumping huge distances without any effort. Although he couldn't see, his other senses guided him. The whole area was alive with sounds and smells. They painted a picture for him; a picture of –

DANGER! He landed on a branch and paused. Something was terribly wrong. His thick, orange fur stood on end. Something bad was about to happen!

A laser blast lit up the woods and turned

the branch beneath Wildmutt to splinters. He leaped for another tree as one of the robot's deadly drones came spinning from the shadows.

With a grunt, the alien launched himself forwards. A sudden heat scorched his back and the tree he'd just swung from exploded in a shower of sparks. He gritted his sharp fangs. **FASTER** – he had to move faster!

Another tree erupted into flame. Wildmutt twisted to avoid the falling trunk. The stench of burning filled his nostrils. He could almost taste the smoke – thick, black and billowing. The perfect place to hide.

The drone slowed to a stop in a clearing and began scanning for any sign of the beast. Its sensors swept over the whole area, but found nothing. Something so large couldn't just vanish. Where could the alien be?

A sound from behind made it spin round. A snarling ball of orange fury sailed through the air, its curved claws outstretched. The flying

disc raised its weapons too late. Wildmutt
landed on it and immediately began to tear it
apart.

His teeth ripped into the drone's electrics.
It shot off through the trees, zigzagging left and
right, desperately trying to shake the beast off.
Wildmutt clung on with one paw and used the
other to claw through the disc's metal body. It
shook and shuddered beneath him. Time to get
off this ride!

Wildmutt jumped from the drone's back
and somersaulted to safety. The watch had
begun to bleep again, and as the spinning

disk exploded against the side of a large rock, the alien transformation wore off. He was Ben again.

'Yesss!' he cheered, spotting the shattered drone. He'd done it! He'd won!

A low humming sound caught Ben's attention. The second robot drone hovered down from the treetops, its weapons trained on him.

'Oh,' Ben gulped. 'Not good.'

CHAPTER FIVE

DIAMOND GEEZER

Ben tried to stumble away, but the drone hovered closer. It detected that the Earthling had the Omnitrix. It switched its weapon systems to full power. One blast would be enough to destroy the human.

It would take only three seconds for its guns to reach maximum strength. Three seconds. Two seconds. One sec –

CLANG! A spade smashed into the drone like an express train. The impact short-circuited its flight systems and it crashed on to the forest floor. It whirred round, scanning for whoever had attacked it. A red-haired girl stood over it, looking down.

'Back off, sparky,' Gwen snarled. She raised her spade and brought it down hard on the drone's robotic disc. 'No flying tree-trimmer is going to hurt my cousin.'

'I never thought I'd say this,' Ben smiled, 'but am I glad to see you!'

When Ben and Gwen were safely back inside The Rust Bucket, Grandpa began his lecture. Ben listened with his head hung low.

'I was worried that you might get popular with that thing on your wrist. That's why I asked you not to fool around with it until we know what the heck it is.'

'Sorry, Grandpa,' Ben said. 'But at least I figured out how to make it work.' He held up his wrist and pointed at the watch. 'All you do is press this button, then when the ring pops up just twist it until you see the guy you want to be. Slam it down and **BAMMO!** You're one of ten super-cool alien dudes!'

'What about staying a "super-cool alien dude" and not transforming back into plain old pizza-face?' Gwen scowled.

'I kinda haven't figured that part out yet,' admitted Ben.

Grandpa gave a sigh. This wasn't the camping trip he had expected.

'With a device as powerful as that watch clamped on you, my guess is we'd better help you learn fast,' he said.

With a loud crackle, The Rust Bucket's short-range radio unexpectedly hissed into life.

'Mayday! Mayday! Somebody help us!' pleaded a frightened voice. 'We're under attack by some sort of . . . I know you're not going to believe me, but *robot*!'

The rest of the transmission was drowned out by static, but it didn't matter. Ben had heard all he needed to hear.

'Sounds just like those things that attacked me,' he said as he stood up. 'It must be looking for the watch. Those people are in trouble because of me.' He took a deep breath and looked up at his grandfather. 'I think I can help them.'

'*You*?' Gwen scoffed. 'What are you gonna do about it, Tennyson?'

Ben threw open The Rust Bucket's door. Gwen and Grandpa followed him as he hurried outside. As he walked, he spun the outside ring of the watch.

'Eenie, meanie, minie . . .' He stopped at one of the alien outlines. 'Here it goes!'

BLEEP! went the watch. Ben's hand slammed down. A now familiar cloud of energy swirled across his body.

'So what can this guy do?' Gwen demanded, once the transformation was complete.

'I don't know.' Ben shrugged. He looked

down at his new body. It sparkled like a precious stone in the moonlight. 'But I bet it's gonna be cool!'

❈ ❈ ❈

At another campsite nearby, Vilgax's robot was destroying everything in its path. Motorhomes and tents exploded as it unleashed power blast after power blast. It had extended to its full height, and now towered like a giant above the wreckage of the camp.

Campers ran, stumbling over each other, trying to get to safety. They screamed as yet more blasts tore the area apart. The robot wanted the Omnitrix, and it was going to find it, no matter what it had to do.

With a clanking of machinery, the android swung an arm down and grabbed one of the fleeing campers. The man screamed and kicked out, struggling to break free of the robot's clutches. It was no use though: the robot was too strong.

'Leave him alone!' boomed a voice from nearby. The robot spun round, searching for the source of the sound.

A large alien, made of what looked like green crystal, stood nearby. It was Ben in the form of the indestructible Diamondhead, and there was no way he was letting anyone get hurt.

'You want somebody to pick on?' he growled. 'Try me!'

Lights blinked behind the robot's eyes as it scanned the newcomer. It dropped the camper to the ground as its targeting system locked on to the watch. It had found the Omnitrix!

A blast of energy screeched from the robot's weapons. It slammed into the ground at Diamondhead's feet, sending the alien tumbling through the air.

With a grinding of metal, Diamondhead crashed through the roof of a motorhome. Another blast from the robot's laser turned the vehicle into a flaming heap of junk, trapping the alien inside. The giant android slowly advanced. That had been almost too easy.

It stopped in its tracks as a razor-sharp hand tore a hole in the burning metal. Diamondhead pulled himself free and studied his arm. As he watched, a dozen deadly spikes grew out from its shiny green surface.

'Cool!' he grinned, before turning his attention back to the matter at hand.

He ran forwards, swinging wildly. This form was built for strength, though not speed, and the robot easily avoided his clumsy attack. It launched itself straight up into the air, before dropping down with its spider-like legs extended.

The metal limbs knocked Diamondhead over and pinned him to the ground. He tried to move, but the robot was too heavy. He was trapped.

'Uhhh . . .' he muttered, 'I think I'm in trouble!'

A short distance away, a park ranger leaped from his car, stunned at what he was seeing.

'What's going on here?' he demanded.

Gwen shouted over her shoulder as she ran past, 'You probably wouldn't believe me if I told you!'

The ranger opened his mouth to answer, but instead screamed with fright as his car was crushed by a falling alien. Diamondhead pulled himself up from the wreckage and gave his head a shake. He was dazed. If he could just take a moment to recover, he'd –

No time! He threw himself clear, just before a power blast turned the car into an oily spot on the ground.

Before Diamondhead could get back to his feet, the robot wrapped a huge, metal claw round him and lifted him high into the air. Another claw wrapped round his arm. He felt a sharp pain shoot through his shoulder as the android gave a violent tug. Diamondhead gasped as he realised what was happening.

The robot was tearing him apart!

CHAPTER SIX

A TASTE OF THEIR OWN MEDICINE

Diamondhead gritted his teeth. The pain was almost too much to bear. If he didn't do something fast, his arm was going to be ripped clean off!

Concentrating hard, he forced shards of diamond to extend out from his trapped arm. They tore through the robot's metal claw, damaging the wiring inside. The android staggered backwards as its arm exploded.

The hand holding Diamondhead fired a piercing power blast, sending him hurtling towards a toilet block. The brick walls crumbled as he smashed through them, head first.

'Ben!' shouted Grandpa helplessly.

But Ben wasn't done for yet. He stumbled from what was left of the toilet block and approached the robot. This fight wasn't over!

He threw up his arms to protect himself as the android launched another power blast. The beam hit his shiny diamond surface and bounced off in every direction. Grandpa, Gwen and the other campers were forced to duck and dodge to avoid the spray of blasts.

Diamondhead watched the beams reflect off his body. His polished surface acted almost like a mirror. That gave him an idea!

'Come on,' he barked, pointing to his chest, 'burn one in here.'

Gwen and Grandpa couldn't believe their ears. Was Ben really inviting the robot to blast him?

'Get out of there!' Grandpa cried. 'Run!'

Diamondhead ignored him. There was no

way he was going to run. He had a plan!

The robot fired his weapon. As the energy crackled towards him, Diamondhead held up his hands. They glowed white hot under the force of the blast.

'Let's see how *you* like it, you techno freak!' he growled.

With a roar of effort, Diamondhead pushed back against the blast, deflecting its deadly beam. The laser curved wildly. It cut a trench in the rocky ground and sliced several trees in half, but with one final effort the alien

directed it towards its real target.

The beam sliced the robot neatly in two. As the top half slid to the ground, the bottom shuddered and shook. Twin explosions ripped through both broken parts, destroying them from the inside out.

'All right!' cheered Grandpa. 'Way to go, Be—' He stopped, realising all the other campers were watching him. Maybe it'd be best if they didn't know who had *really* saved the day. 'Uh . . . diamond-headed guy.'

'Oh, yeah! Who's bad?' Diamondhead laughed. He twisted his arms and shook his butt in a dance of celebration. The campers stared at him. Was this guy crazy? 'Well,' he coughed, noticing their looks, 'I think my work here is done.'

And, with that, he ran off into the woods, as fast as his indestructible legs would carry him.

�֍ �֍ ✖

Floating inside his life-support tube, Vilgax was furious. He had been following events on his ship's view screen. Things had not gone according to plan.

'Failure,' he scowled. 'Unbelievable! The puny Earth-being that is keeping the Omnitrix from me will soon hang on my trophy wall!'

His red eyes grew dark and narrow. It would take time for him to heal, but heal he would. Soon he would make the boy pay. Soon he would make the whole pathetic planet pay!

He looked down at the stumps where his legs should be.

Soon, but not quite yet . . .

* * *

The next morning, Grandpa and Gwen were packing up The Rust Bucket and preparing to move on. Grandpa finished loading a box into the motorhome and looked around. Something was missing.

'Where's Ben?'

Gwen shrugged. 'I haven't seen him since breakfast.'

A sudden wind whipped up from nowhere and tore through the camp. Grandpa stepped back in surprise as a sleek, blue-and-black alien named XLR8 skidded to a halt right beside him.

'Ben?'

'Yup,' the alien replied. 'Hey, check this out!'

Grandpa and Gwen blinked in surprise. They'd hardly noticed the alien move, but suddenly all their belongings were stacked neatly inside The Rust Bucket.

'Pretty fast, huh?' beamed Ben in his alien form.

With a **BLEEP BLEEP BLEEP BLEEEEP!** and a blinding flash, the alien turned back into plain old Ben Tennyson.

'I think this is going to be the best summer ever,' he grinned.

'Absolutely,' nodded Grandpa Max.

'It's definitely going to be interesting,' Gwen agreed. 'So, where'd you go, anyway?'

'Just had to take care of a few things,' he smirked.

※ ※ ※

Back in the playground of Ben's school, two bullies found themselves dangling from a tree by their underwear. How had they got there? Neither one of them had any idea. What they did know was that whatever it was that had happened to them had happened very, *very* fast!

※ ※ ※

Ben couldn't help but chuckle as he took his seat in The Rust Bucket. That robot wasn't the only one to have been given a taste of its own medicine!

He leaned back, his hands behind his head, as Grandpa started the engine. Ben wasn't sure what adventures lay ahead, or what other surprises the watch had in store for him. He knew one thing for certain though – it was going to be a whole lot of fun finding out!

VILGAX IS ON A MISSION
TO FIND THE OMNITRIX

WHILE BEN'S ON A MISSION
TO ANNOY HIS COUSIN!

IS IT A BIRD? IS IT A PLANE?

NOPE – IT'S THE OMNITRIX!

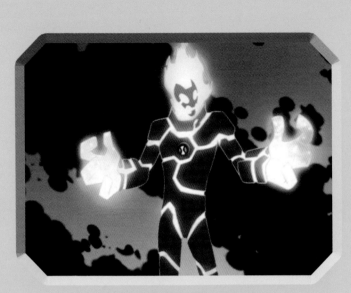

NOW THINGS ARE REALLY
HOTTING UP FOR BEN!

HE GOES WILD(MUTT) FOR VILGAX'S DRONE

DIAMONDHEAD CUTS THE ENEMY
DOWN TO SIZE

AND XLR8'S CLEAN-UP OPERATION
PUTS THINGS RIGHT

GHOSTFREAK GETS HIS HANDS
ON A GAMES CONSOLE

BUT BEN ENDS UP CAUGHT IN THE ACT!

BEN MAKES A TOKEN 'FRIEND'
DOWN AT THE ARCADE

AND GOES ALIEN TO HELP THEM
ESCAPE THE LAW

BUT THE POLICE ARE SOON IN HOT PURSUIT

WHEN KEVIN SAPS BEN'S ENERGY
THE RIDE GETS BUMPY

BUT FOUR ARMS GETS TO GRIPS
WITH THE SITUATION

AND KEVIN 11 IS LEFT EMPTY-HANDED

CHAPTER ONE

THE BIG APPLE

The skyscrapers of New York City stretched high above Ben, Grandpa and Gwen as they passed through the entrance of a large hotel. The cousins were excited – they had been sleeping in The Rust Bucket for weeks, but now they were about to book into an actual hotel!

And not just *any* hotel. It was the most luxurious-looking hotel either of them had ever seen. What's more, if the lobby were anything to go by, it was the biggest one they'd ever seen too!

While Grandpa Max spoke with the woman at the check-in desk, Gwen looked through the building's brochure. With every word she read she became more and more excited.

'Wow, this hotel has everything!' she said. 'Indoor pool, spa . . .'

'Now, don't get used to it,' warned Grandpa. 'It's only for one night.'

They picked up their suitcases and began to wheel them across the lobby. Before they were even halfway across, Ben stopped. Something had caught his attention. Something amazing!

'Whoa!' he cried, dropping his case. A sign hanging above a nearby door showed one of the characters from *Sumo Slammers*, Ben's favourite TV show.

Ben ran towards the door. The latest video game based on the show wasn't out for months, but a sneak preview was taking place on the other side of that door. He had to get in – nothing was going to stop him!

A large security guard stopped him. He

loomed above Ben, muscles bulging under his black suit.

'Pass?' he growled.

Ben pretended to search through his pockets. 'Must've left it inside,' he smiled. 'I'm one of the game pros testing out the system.'

Ben grinned confidently and folded his arms. The guard would definitely fall for that one.

'VIPs only.'

OK, so maybe he wouldn't fall for it. Ben

turned and slunk back to Grandpa and Gwen with his head hung low.

'I know what you're thinking,' Grandpa Max whispered. 'So no sneaking back in there.'

'I won't,' Ben sighed. He hung back, watching Grandpa and Gwen drag their bags across to the elevator. *He* wouldn't sneak in, but he knew an alien who would!

After a quick check to make sure no one was watching, Ben activated the Omnitrix. A cloud of energy swirled over him, transforming him into the terrifying Ghostfreak!

Making himself invisible, Ghostfreak floated silently past the security guard and through the closed doors.

The room he emerged into was *Sumo Slammers* heaven! Posters and cardboard cut-outs of the characters lined the walls. Ghostfreak barely even noticed. Instead he floated straight for a games console that was set up in the middle of the room.

69

'The ultimate sneak peek,' he whispered, picking up a controller, 'for the ghost with the most freak!'

Out in the lobby, Grandpa and Gwen paused at the elevator. Something was wrong. Something was missing . . .

'Ben?' said Grandpa. He turned round and sighed. Ben was nowhere to be seen.

✖ ✖ ✖

'Yes!' Ben cheered. 'New high score!'

On screen, a huge sumo wrestler performed a dance of celebration. Over Ben's shoulder, an equally large shape slowly stepped forwards.

'What've you got to say for yourself, kid?' snarled the security guard.

Ben looked down at the Omnitrix and

gasped. In the excitement of playing, he hadn't noticed the transformation wearing off. He was no longer Ghostfreak, which meant he was no longer invisible.

He looked up at the guard and smiled nervously. 'Ah . . . "game over"?'

Grandpa's suitcase hit the pavement with a thud. He looked down at it sadly.

'And never come back!' warned the

security guard. He growled at Ben one more time before pushing his way back into the hotel.

Grandpa, Ben and Gwen all bent down together and picked up their cases. The wheels squeaked as they pulled them along the street in the direction of The Rust Bucket.

'I told you not to sneak in there!' said Grandpa.

'Well, if you want to get all "technical" about it!'

'I never even got a chance to take a shower!' complained Gwen. 'In a *real* shower, for the first time all summer. Plus they had a spa! A *spa!*' She sighed and turned away from her cousin. 'Nice going, doofus.'

They arrived at The Rust Bucket and clambered inside. It felt even smaller now than it usually did.

'How do you expect me to trust you if you keep misusing the watch?' Grandpa asked.

'Excuse me! I've used it a hundred times

for good,' Ben protested. 'Why can't I use it just once for me?'

'It's not how *many* times you use it, Ben, it's *how* you use it.'

Ben shrugged. 'It was no big deal.'

'To you. And that's all you care about,' glowered Grandpa. 'So no more *Sumo Slammers* stuff for two weeks. No comics, no trading cards . . .'

'No fair!' cried Ben.

'Neither's getting booted from a four-star hotel I already paid for!'

'Fine. Take it out of my allowance!'

'You don't get an allowance,' Gwen reminded him.

'Stay out of this!' snapped Ben and Grandpa together.

Ben scowled. 'This is my vacation too! You can't always tell me what to do. You're not my dad.'

'Well, if I were . . .' Grandpa began. He

stopped and shook his head. Arguing was
getting them nowhere. 'Look, I'm going back
in the hotel to see if I can get at least some of
my money back,' he said. 'I'll be back in a few
minutes.'

'Don't hurry,' muttered Ben. He stormed
off to the back of The Rust Bucket and pulled
the dividing door over with a slam.

'He'll be fine,' Gwen told Grandpa. He
nodded, then climbed out of the motorhome and

headed back towards the hotel.

'Not fair! Not fair! Totally not fair!' moaned Ben. He kicked the thin door, making it shake.

'Glad to hear you're handling things so maturely,' said Gwen as Ben slid the door open again. He pushed past her, making his way towards the exit. 'Where do you think you're going?' she demanded.

'Where does it look like? Out.'

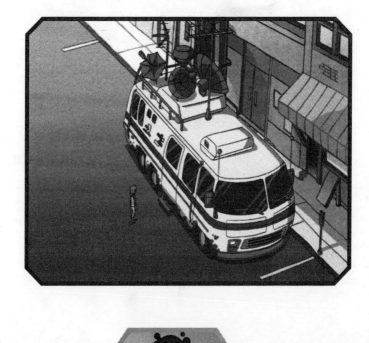

He jumped down from The Rust Bucket and marched off along the street, away from the hotel. Gwen hopped down after him.

'Get back here!'

'Sorry,' Ben snapped. 'I don't speak dweeb.'

Gwen watched him walk away, then decided to follow. There was no saying what he'd get up to if he were left on his own. 'You,' she sighed, 'are going to be so grounded!'

Ben walked for several minutes, not really sure where he was going. After a few twists and turns, he rounded a corner and found himself standing outside a video arcade called 'The Total Zone'. A smile broke out across his face. This would be the perfect place to chill out.

Without hesitating, he ducked through the doorway and into the arcade. Gwen paused outside, listening to the bleeping, beeping and chiming of hundreds of video games. She shook her head.

'Next summer,' she sighed, 'I'm going to sleep-away camp.'

CHAPTER TWO

A NEW FRIEND?

Ben wandered through The Total Zone with eyes as wide as saucers. Everywhere he looked he saw something unbelievably cool. Every type of games machine he could think of was in this place, and the only problem he had was deciding which one to try first.

At last, he settled on a baseball simulator. He stepped on to the sensor plate, picked up the bat and dropped his coins into the slot. On the monitor, an animated pitcher stepped up and prepared to throw the ball.

Ben tightened his grip on the bat, getting ready to knock the ball out of the on-screen park. As the pitcher wound up his arm to throw, the picture shuddered and then froze. Ben watched with horror as the words 'Game Over' flashed up on the screen.

'Game over?' He frowned. 'It just started.' He spotted an attendant strolling past. 'This thing just ate my tokens!' he complained.

'Read the sign, kid,' shrugged the attendant. 'It says "Play at your own risk".'

'This place is a rip off! Know that?!'

Over by another machine, a boy with long black hair watched on with interest.

'You're right,' he said. 'The games here stink.'

'Yeah, but not as bad as his breath,' said Ben, still watching the attendant. '*Major* case of sewer mouth.'

The boy laughed. 'You're funny,' he smiled. 'Here. You owe me one.'

He rested a hand on one of the machines. A wave of blue energy crackled from his fingertips. Almost at once, hundreds of tokens

poured out from inside the cabinet.

'*Whoa!* How'd you do that?'

'I've got some skills.'

Ben bent down and scooped up handfuls of the shiny tokens. There were enough here to keep him playing for months!

'We can't take those,' said Gwen, suddenly appearing behind him. 'They're not ours.'

'They are now,' Ben replied. 'Thanks,' he said to the boy. 'I'm Ben.'

'Kevin.'

'Wanna play some air hockey?'

Kevin opened his mouth to say 'yes', then closed it again. Four teenagers were pushing their way through the crowds in his direction.

'Nuh. Gotta bail,' Kevin said. He turned and walked away quickly.

'He's total trouble,' Gwen warned.

'He seemed OK to me,' replied Ben, before one of the gang members shoved him out of the way. He watched them close in on Kevin. His new friend was in trouble.

'Long time no see,' snarled an evil-looking thug as he stepped out in front of Kevin. 'Where you going, freak? Home to recharge your batteries?'

Kevin backed away, but two other gang members caught him by the arms and held him in place. He was trapped!

'Need some help?' asked Ben.

'Huh,' scoffed the leader. 'He's going

to need a lot more than you. Now beat it.' He pushed Ben hard in the chest, sending him tumbling backwards on to the ground.

Ben leaped back to his feet. 'I've got some skills too,' he muttered.

Ducking behind another arcade cabinet, he gave the Omnitrix's dials a twist. He wanted to take care of these thugs quickly, and when it came to doing things quickly, there was one alien he could always rely on.

'So how's the hangout?' Kevin sneered at the gang leader. 'Still trashed like I left it for you?'

'Yeah, and you're gonna pay! You can't take us all alone, freak!'

'But *I* can!'

A strange figure stepped from behind an arcade machine. Ben had transformed into the ultra-fast XLR8!

'Little early for Halloween, dude, isn't it?' cackled one of the gang members.

In a blinding blur of speed, XLR8 shot towards the group. He circled them, running faster and faster, until the gang leader was lifted off the ground by a mini tornado. He screamed as the whirlwind spun him round and round.

As suddenly as he had started, XLR8 stopped. The gang leader hung in the air for a second, frantically flapping his arms in an attempt to stop himself falling.

It was no use. His screams continued as he dropped like a stone back towards the arcade floor. Just before he hit, XLR8 flicked out his tail. It struck the thug on the side and slammed him hard against the nearest wall. He let out a low groan as he slid slowly to the ground.

XLR8 shot off around the arcade. The gang members tried to follow him with their eyes, but the alien was far too fast.

'Where'd he go?' whimpered one of them. A streak of speed lifted him off his feet and

crunched him down on top of the gang's boss.
Another of the thugs quickly found himself
hurtling headlong towards the pile. Then
another, and another.

In the blink of an eye, all five members of
the gang were stacked up against a wall. They
groaned quietly, not sure what had hit them,
but certain they didn't want it to happen again.

XLR8 screeched to a halt next to Kevin.
He fired off a friendly salute, and then rocketed
away to find cover before the transformation
wore off.

�֎ ✖ ✖

A few minutes later, Gwen joined Ben outside
The Total Zone. She scowled at him, her hands
on her hips.

'I can't believe you went alien!'

'He helped me, so I helped him. You
wouldn't get it. And neither would Grandpa,'

Ben snapped. 'That's the problem.'

'You see what that speed guy did to those losers?' cried Kevin, emerging from inside the arcade.

'Yeah,' Ben smiled. 'Dude's name is XLR8. In fact, we're pretty tight.'

'Cool! Hey, want a tour of New York?'

'You keep Grandpa waiting any longer he's going to pop another gasket. We gotta go.' Gwen stared at her cousin through narrowed eyes. 'Like *now*, Ben.'

Ben snorted. 'Don't you mean *you* have to go?'

Gwen shook her head, but realised there was nothing she could say that would change his mind. 'You're on your own,' she sighed, walking off.

'Good. That's the way I want it.' Ben turned his back on his cousin and followed Kevin through the back streets of New York City.

'So how'd you get your power?' Ben asked after a while.

'I was born with it,' Kevin explained. 'I'm like an energy sponge. Motors, air conditioners, lights, batteries, whatever. Soak it up, then dish it out when I have to.' He grinned wickedly. 'Or want to.'

'Cool!'

'Come on,' said Kevin. 'I'll show you where I live.'

He led Ben through unfamiliar streets and alleyways until they reached a boarded-up entrance to an old subway station. Kevin pulled a plank of wood to the side, making room for Ben to squeeze through.

The station had been abandoned for years, but for Kevin it was home. Broken furniture lay scattered about, alongside some high-tech TV and computer game equipment. A huge *Sumo Slammers* cut-out stood guard next to the gadgets. Ben thought it may well have been the coolest place he had ever seen!

'You live here?' asked Ben.

'Yeah, by myself.'

'What about your family?'

'Long gone.' Kevin shrugged. 'They weren't too thrilled at having a freak for a son. But it just means I don't answer to nobody.'

'Sounds good to me. So why was that gang after you?'

'I kinda trashed their hangout under the Thirty-Ninth Street bridge,' explained Kevin. 'What about you? Sounds like your grandpa's pretty steamed at you.'

'Like usual,' Ben sighed. 'And all I did was sneak in and play the new *Sumo Slammers* computer game.'

'The one that won't be out until Christmas?' Kevin asked.

'Yeah.'

Kevin's mouth curled into a grin. He had an idea!

※ ※ ※

'I got a tip a new shipment just came in,' whispered Kevin. He had led Ben down to the docks, and now they were crouching in the shadows outside an old warehouse.

After checking the coast was clear, Kevin sneaked up to the door. It was locked. An electronic keypad was mounted on the wall next to it. Any normal person would need a code to get inside, but then Kevin wasn't any normal person.

The keypad sparked and fizzled as Kevin held his hand over it. With a **CLUNK** the lock slid open, and the two boys stepped into the warehouse. Neither of them noticed the light of a security alarm begin to blink as they entered.

Rows and rows of wooden boxes were stacked up inside the warehouse. Kevin walked over to one and prised the lid open. With a flick of his wrist, he tossed Ben a copy of the brand-new *Sumo Slammers* game.

'Check it out! Wait's over, dude,' Kevin grinned.

'Yesss!' cheered Ben, before the sound of shattering glass caught his attention. He looked up in time to see four metal cylinders come crashing through the windows. Even before they hit the ground, the canisters had begun to spray clouds of choking tear gas everywhere.

With a screeching of tyres and blaring of sirens, a squad of police cars skidded to a stop outside the warehouse. Overhead, Ben could hear helicopters swooping closer. His stomach tightened into a knot as he realised that he and Kevin were completely surrounded!

CHAPTER THREE

SHOO, FLY, SHOO!

Ben coughed. The tear gas was filling the warehouse. They didn't have much time.

'What do we do?' he wheezed.

'Get outta here!'

They ran. Spotting a power socket, Kevin stopped. He touched the outlet and a surge of energy shot along his arm. The warehouse was lit by a bright blue light as Kevin drained all the power he needed.

A set of wide double doors exploded inwards, and two policemen came running in. They both wore masks to protect them from the gas, and each one held a powerful rifle.

'Freeze, punks!' they yelled.

Kevin clambered up into the driver's
seat of a forklift truck. For a moment, his hand
glowed with energy. The forklift spluttered,
then roared into life.

'Time to rev things up!'

With a wave of his hand, Kevin sent
the forklift speeding forwards. It trapped the
policemen against a stack of wooden crates.

'Let's go!' Kevin cried. He and Ben
sprinted to the exit, only for a police car to block
the way. They ran in the other direction, but
another car pulled up in front of them.

'Great,' groaned Ben as they both ducked
behind a large crate. 'No way out.'

'Any ideas?' asked Kevin.

Ben glanced down at the watch. He knew
he shouldn't do this, but . . .

'Only one,' he said. 'But can you keep a
secret?'

'Sure.'

Ben twisted the dial on the Omnitrix,

searching for the one alien he knew could get them out of this mess.

'What are you doing with your watch?' Kevin frowned.

Ben didn't answer. Instead, he slammed his hand, triggering another transformation.

Energy swirled out from the watch and began to change him.

Four antennae eyes pushed out from the side of his head, just as an extra pair of legs sprouted from his hips. Huge insect wings burst out from his back, completing the transformation. Ben had become the alien Stinkfly.

'Uh! You reek!' Kevin winced.

'I know!'

Outside, a dozen policemen edged towards the doors. They were sent tumbling like skittles as a green shape shot straight through the middle of them. Helplessly, they watched it soar off across the water.

❈ ❈ ❈

Stinkfly swooped down low over the waves, carrying Kevin below him. The boy could hardly believe what was happening.

'Oh, yeah! And people call *me* a freak. How'd you do that?'

'Talk later,' hissed Stinkfly. He'd spotted a squadron of police helicopters close behind.

The alien insect dodged just in time to avoid a sudden burst of machine-gun fire.

Stinkfly banked upwards, trying to shake off their pursuers. He zoomed up towards the Statue of Liberty, which towered above the New York harbour.

Two of the police helicopters swung round the statue's left side. They met the third, which had flown round on the right. Their target was nowhere to be seen.

'Where'd they go?' barked one of the pilots.

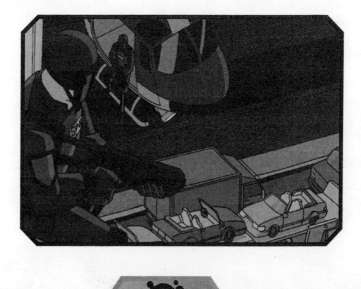

Down below one of the helicopters, Stinkfly and Kevin clung tightly on. If they moved, they would be seen, but they didn't have much choice.

'I'm running out of time,' Stinkfly warned. 'I'll lose them in the city.'

Catching hold of Kevin, Stinkfly dropped down from the underside of the helicopter. The rat-tat-tat of machine-gun fire followed him as he sped down towards New York.

The helicopters were quickly catching up. Stinkfly kept as low to the ground as he could, dodging in and out of traffic, making things as difficult as possible for the pilots. They wouldn't dare open fire in such a crowded place.

A spray of bullets ricocheted off the road just a few metres from Stinkfly's head. The police weren't holding back. They were shooting to kill!

Zipping left and right, Stinkfly weaved his way through the city streets. No matter which way he turned, the helicopters followed. No matter how fast he flew, they got steadily closer.

This was bad. *Really* bad.

Stinkfly didn't notice The Rust Bucket as he swooped over the top of it, but Gwen and Grandpa noticed him – and the helicopters chasing him. They watched in horror until he flew round a corner and out of sight.

'Can't shake 'em!' Stinkfly gasped. The three helicopters had rounded the bend behind him, and were lining up their next shots. He spotted a huge car transporter about to drive under a road bridge below. 'I've got an idea,' he buzzed.

All three pilots watched the insect fly down towards the transporter. It was too close to the bridge for them to get in front of it. They'd catch it on the other side.

When the truck drove out from under the bridge, there was no sign of the creature they had been chasing. Instead, two boys sat in one of the cars, enjoying the ride.

'Where'd that thing go?' demanded a
pilot. The others could only scratch their heads.
Whatever that monster was, it had somehow
managed to get away.

✖ ✖ ✖

A little later, Ben walked along a dirty alleyway,
with Kevin bouncing excitedly at his side.

'So that watch lets you be that dragonfly thing whenever you want?' he quizzed.

'And not just that one,' boasted Ben. 'It sends out this special energy so I can turn into ten different aliens.'

'*Ten?* So the speed guy at the arcade was you?' He pointed at Ben and grinned. 'You're the man! Show me what other aliens you can morph into.'

'It's not that simple.' Ben shrugged. 'It has a mind of its own.'

'Gimme it,' Kevin demanded. 'Maybe I can make it work.'

'Can't. It's stuck on my wrist.'

Kevin stared at the watch for a few moments before a thought occurred to him.

'We should be partners,' he said. 'Between the two of us, with our powers, we could do what we want, whenever we want. I mean totally cash in. What do you say? Huh?' He held his hand out to Ben. 'Friends?'

Ben hesitated, but then took hold of Kevin's hand and gave it a shake. 'Friends,' he said with a nod.

* * *

The Rust Bucket sped through the streets of the city, dodging in and out of traffic. On board, Gwen held on to her seat as Grandpa pushed the accelerator pedal hard against the floor.

'Of all the stunts Ben's pulled, this is the worst,' Grandpa growled. 'When I find him . . .'

Gwen gulped. She'd never seen her grandfather quite this mad before. She wouldn't like to be in Ben's shoes when they caught up with him.

'I should really be enjoying this,' she sighed. 'So why aren't I?'

* * *

Kevin and Ben hopped over a gate and landed on the platform of an empty subway station. It looked almost exactly like the one Kevin lived in, except it was much cleaner. The lights dangling down from overhead were all switched on, meaning the station was still in regular use.

'Gimme a boost,' said Kevin, looking up at one of the lights. 'I need to recharge.'

Ben took hold of his friend's foot and lifted him towards the light fitting. Blue waves of energy washed over Kevin as he soaked up the electrical power.

Once he was fully charged, Kevin hopped down on to the tracks and crossed to a lever that stuck up from the ground. As he took hold of the handle, a bolt of energy passed along it. A section of track slowly rotated. It locked into a new position with a **CLANK**.

'What are we doing?' asked Ben.

'A money train loaded with cash comes down this track,' explained Kevin excitedly.

'So when it crashes into the oncoming passenger train – **BOOM!** – instant jackpot! You turn into that XLR8 guy and we're outta here!'

Ben gasped. He couldn't believe what he was hearing. 'But hundreds of innocent people will be killed!'

Kevin's face broke into a wide, wicked grin. 'Hey,' he cackled, 'no pain, no gain!'

CHAPTER FOUR

FRIENDS NO MORE

'You can't do this!' cried Ben.

'Sure we can,' Kevin replied. 'I just switched the tracks!'

Ben bunched his hands into fists. 'I mean, I'm not gonna let you do this.'

'We shook,' snarled Kevin. 'We're partners.'

'No. This is going way too far.'

'Then try and stop me, watch-boy.'

Ben paused, remembering something his Grandpa had said to him. 'You don't care about anyone but yourself,' he whispered.

'You talking about me?' demanded Kevin.

'No,' said Ben. 'I'm talking about me.'

A flash of energy suddenly struck him in the chest. Ben stumbled and tripped over the raised train track.

'You do *not* want to make me mad,' warned Kevin. Coils of energy curled around his hands and flickered along his fingers.

'Me neither,' growled Ben. 'I'm switching the track back.' He gave the Omnitrix a twist. 'Time to go Four Arms!'

With a blinding flash, Ben's transformation began. Something was wrong,

though. He wasn't changing into the super-strong Four Arms after all. Instead, he felt his whole body ignite into a ball of flame as he became Heatblast.

'Stupid watch,' he mumbled. He realised Kevin had seen the entire transformation. 'Move back,' Heatblast commanded.

'Or what? You're going to burn my dinner?'

'Fight me – you're the one who's gonna be burned.'

Kevin threw out an arm and sent electrical energy crackling into the station's power grid. With a series of pops, the overhead lights exploded one by one, plunging the area into near darkness.

Only Heatblast was visible in the gloom. His flames lit him up like a firefly, making him an easy target. Frantically, he looked around for Kevin, but the boy was nowhere to be seen.

A pair of arms wrapped tightly round

Heatblast's neck from behind. Kevin clung on, cackling with delight. It didn't last long. A burst of fiery energy shot up his arm, making him cry out in pain. He dropped from the alien's back and rolled clumsily to safety.

Heatblast spun round, searching for Kevin. Even though Kevin had attacked him, he still felt bad for burning him. Something shone brightly in the nearby shadows and Heatblast stepped closer to take a look.

A ball of spinning flame hit him in the chest, knocking him over as if he were a skittle. The alien lay on the ground for a moment, catching his breath.

He gasped as something that wasn't quite Kevin stepped from the darkness. Much of the villain looked the same as ever, but his head and one arm now looked exactly like Heatblast himself!

Kevin laughed. 'I absorb energy, remember?'

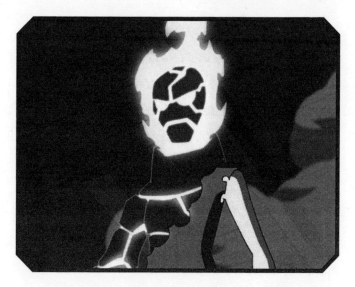

'You don't have to do this!' said Heatblast, leaping to his feet. He threw himself at Kevin, but the boy was too fast. As Heatblast stumbled past, Kevin struck him on the back with another fireball, sending him crashing on to the tracks.

'It's time I got what's coming to me,' cried Kevin. 'No one's calling me "freak" any more!'

Down on the ground, Heatblast wasn't listening. His muscles ached and his head was spinning; Kevin's energy drain had taken a lot out of him.

He was about to pull himself up when he heard a rumble in the distance. It was low and quiet, but getting steadily louder. A light appeared down one of the tunnels. A train was coming.

Heatblast whipped his head round as another sound echoed from the tunnel in the opposite direction. A second light sliced through the dark. Kevin had been right – the trains were going to crash!

The flames behind Kevin's eyes lit up even brighter when he spotted the speeding trains. 'Payday!' he grinned.

Heatblast knew he only had one chance. Reaching out an arm, he launched a jet of flame at the handle, switching the tracks. The fire made the metal glow white-hot. The trains were almost upon him though. Would there be enough time?

A split second before the trains collided, the lever melted, switching the tracks back to their original position. Heatblast felt a wind whip at him as the passenger train sped harmlessly past. He let out a sigh of relief.

He'd saved the day!

But his happiness was short-lived; a horn blasted behind him and he turned round. The money train was speeding straight for him! A tower of flame erupted from the alien before the train thundered across the spot where he had stood.

Kevin watched a wall of fire lick at the front of the train for a few moments, before it faded away. He looked around, but Ben was nowhere to be seen. The train must have finished him off.

So the plan to derail the money train had failed. All that cash: gone. Kevin was disappointed, but he tried to put it from his mind for the moment.

'Forget the money,' he hissed, leaping over the gate that led to the exit. 'Time to get some priceless revenge.'

The money train hurtled along the tracks, trying to make up for lost time. On board, the driver tried not to think too much about the flaming figure he'd seen standing in the middle of the tracks. It had been a trick of the light, that was all. Nothing to worry about.

Meanwhile, less than a metre above the driver's head, Heatblast clung on to the train's shiny metal roof. His fiery fingers slid on the slippery surface. The wind whooshed past, making it difficult to keep his eyes open, and threatening to blow out his flame. His grip slipped on the roof and he skidded back along the train.

He bounced hard on the last carriage and felt the roof slip past beneath him. Instinctively, he blasted the metal with a mini fireball, creating a hole just the right size for his hand. Heatblast forced his fingers inside and held on for all he was worth.

Now he had a handhold he could relax. In his alien form he was strong enough to keep his grip, and there was bound to be a station coming up soon. The train would stop and he would hop off. What could possibly go wrong?

BLEEP BLEEP BLEEP BLEEEEP! The watch flashed a worrying shade of red. Realising what was about to happen, Heatblast sighed.

'Oh, man, I hate that sound!'

❋ ❋ ❋

The Rust Bucket skidded round a bend, narrowly avoiding crashing into a hotdog stand. In the passenger seat, Gwen fiddled with the short-range radio, trying to pick up emergency-service broadcasts. With a crackle of static, they began receiving a transmission.

'. . . and expect delays on the uptown subway lines near Fifty-First Street,' warned the announcer. 'There have been reports of fires breaking out all over the tunnels.'

'Grandpa!' Gwen gasped.

Grandpa Max nodded and spun the wheel. 'I know!'

❈ ❈ ❈

On top of the train, Ben was finding it more and more difficult to hang on. The track had emerged from underground and was now travelling on a raised bridge alongside the city streets. The speed and strength of the wind in his face almost choked him. Its icy chill nipped at his knuckles, forcing him to loosen his grip. Any moment now he was going to slip.

The honking of a horn caught his attention. The Rust Bucket was speeding along beside the train. As Ben watched, a soft shade canopy extended from the side of the motorhome. If he could land on that, he'd be safe.

Ben took a deep breath and got ready to leap. He'd only have one chance. If he missed, then . . .

He shook his head. Missing wasn't an option.

Closing his eyes and gritting his teeth, Ben let go of his handhold – and jumped.

CHAPTER FIVE

SIX ARMS ARE BETTER THAN FOUR

With a grunt, Ben thudded against the canopy. He was thrown around wildly, and for a moment he thought he was going to bounce right off. Gradually, The Rust Bucket slowed down, and Ben was able to get a better grip.

'None of this would have happened if you'd just obeyed me from the beginning!' snapped Grandpa, when Ben was back inside the motorhome. 'It's all about trust.'

'Then trust me that Kevin's probably misusing Heatblast's power right now!' replied Ben.

'OK,' Grandpa sighed, 'so where is he?'

Ben thought hard. What did he know about Kevin? Where would he go? What would he –? Of course!

'I think I know,' said Ben gravely. He turned the Omnitrix's dial. 'Going Stinkfly. See you at the Thirty-Ninth Street bridge!'

With a flash of energy, Ben transformed into an enormous red-skinned alien. He was so big he could barely fit in the back of The Rust Bucket.

'Great,' he muttered. '*Now* I turn into Four Arms!'

❈ ❈ ❈

In their hideout under the Thirty-Ninth Street bridge, a familiar gang of boys were having the worst night of their lives. They scrambled away from Kevin, trying to avoid the fireballs he hurled at them.

'Kevin, we can work this out!' begged the leader.

'I don't think so,' Kevin snarled. With a blast of his heat powers he brought a section of the bridge crashing down. It landed on top of the gang, trapping them underneath.

Kevin raised his arm and pointed it towards the trapped boys. An evil smile crept across his face.

'So much for your gang!'

With a sudden **WHOOSH**, Kevin's Heatblast energy faded away, leaving him normal once again. He stared down at his hands, confused.

'What's going on?' he demanded.

'Your power's gone,' boomed a voice from behind him. Four Arms landed on the concrete, cracking it into pieces.

'Looks like you're about to give me some more, Ben.'

'No.'

Kevin leaped up on to the fallen rubble and held his hands over the heads of the gang members. Energy crackled from his palms.

'You don't have a choice,' Kevin smirked. 'I've still got enough juice to fry these guys.'

Four Arms stepped forwards and

snatched Kevin up before he could hurt anyone. He didn't realise he'd walked right into his enemy's trap.

Kevin pressed his hands against the alien's arms and felt a wave of energy surge through his body. He laughed as he soaked up Ben's alien power. He could feel himself getting stronger with every second that passed.

He threw an elbow back, smashing Four Arms in the face. The alien released his grip, letting the boy slide to the ground. When Kevin stood back up, he had transformed into a twisted version of the four-armed red giant.

Roaring, Kevin thundered forwards. As he ran, another pair of arms sprouted from his shoulders! He drew one back and lashed out with a punch. It caught Four Arms under the chin and set him crashing through a stack of concrete blocks.

Kevin cracked all six sets of knuckles at once. 'This is gonna be real fun!'

'Tell me about it,' Four Arms replied, getting back to his feet.

He ducked, avoiding a flurry of wild punches from Kevin. Moving fast, Four Arms caught his opponent by the wrists, and the two giants began to grapple each other.

'I'm taking all your alien powers!' Kevin

growled. His two extra arms caught Four Arms by the throat and slammed him hard against a wall. While the alien was still dazed, Kevin jerked him off the ground, then drove his head down into the concrete.

Up on the bridge, Grandpa and Gwen leaped from The Rust Bucket and rushed down to where the fight was taking place. There was nothing they could do to help Ben – Kevin was too strong, but they could help the trapped gang.

'Moving day,' Grandpa told them as he cleared away the rubble. 'Get out!'

The gang didn't need telling twice. Not daring to look back, they all took to their heels and fled into the night.

A moment later, a flailing mass of limbs hit the side of the bridge like a cannonball. Kevin and Four Arms were locked in battle, each driving powerful punches into their opponent.

Without warning, the Omnitrix started to flash and **BLEEP!** Four Arms stared at it in horror. The transformation was about to wear off!

Realising he had no time to lose, he gave it everything he had. Fast, furious punches rained down on Kevin's head, dazing him. Four Arms slammed his feet against Kevin's chest. As the six-armed mutant staggered backwards, Four Arms followed up with a devastating shoulder-slam. It flipped Kevin end over end, and sent him crashing into one of the bridge's support pillars.

'C'mon, I give. I give. I'm sorry!' Kevin wailed, struggling to get free of a mound of rubble that had collapsed on to him. 'Please, just lighten up!'

'I just did,' announced Ben, who was now back in human form. 'By about three hundred pounds.'

'Guess I just went too wild with power,' whimpered Kevin. 'I don't have anyone else like you to help me.'

'We can still be partners,' Ben offered. 'We'd just be kicking butt for good instead of for ourselves.'

Kevin considered this. 'What's in it for me?'

'For starters, people will like you.' Ben

stretched out his hand. Kevin stared at it for a long time, before reaching out to accept the offer of friendship.

Or so Ben thought. Instead of shaking his hand, Kevin grabbed Ben by the wrist and lifted him so his feet were dangling in mid-air.

'Oh, man! You are so dim,' Kevin cackled. 'Now give me the watch!' He took hold of the Omnitrix and gave it a tug. It was stuck fast.

'You're the one who's dim. I told you I can't take it off!'

Kevin gave the watch another pull. As he did, a bolt of bright green energy surged from inside the device. The blast launched them both in opposite directions. Ben hurtled safely into his grandpa's arms, while Kevin smashed through another bridge support. With a hideous grinding of concrete and metal, the bridge crumpled and collapsed on top of him.

When Kevin pulled himself free, he no longer had six arms. He didn't even have four. Instead, he was back to being his old self – something he wasn't too pleased about at all.

'Nooo!' he screamed, and then, before anyone could stop him, he turned and fled into the dark back alleys of the city.

'I'm sorry, Grandpa,' said Ben. 'For everything.'

Grandpa Max nodded solemnly. 'I know you are. You're my grandson, and nothing will ever change that.' He turned away and walked back towards The Rust Bucket. 'But my trust is something you'll have to earn back.'

Ben watched his grandpa go. He'd learned a lot about trust today. He'd prove to Grandpa Max that he was trustworthy, even if it took all summer.

�֎ �֎ ✖

In an abandoned subway station, a misshapen figure sat hidden by shadow. He could feel something happening to him. Something was changing.

'If they thought I was a freak before,' Kevin hissed, 'just wait!'

As a flickering flame sprung up from his hand, Kevin laughed. The sound echoed around the station before being swallowed forever by the darkness.